In JFK's Terminal A, Gate 33, Myles watches a stranger push slim fingers through tangled blonde hair. He wants to sit in the open seat next to her, but his diffidence triumphs, and he hops the terminal's moving walkway to the nearest magazine shop. A quick scan for indulgences, and inspiration strikes: He buys a packet of Skittles to be used to invite conversation with a "Want one?" hello.

Back at Gate 33, he weaves toward her, but once he's steps away, his sugary, pre-flight introduction is postponed indefinitely: she rips open a Family Size bag of M&M's.

The M&M's star as a placebo to Nicole's aviophobia. She's calmed by the candy shell's shatter, the chocolate release, the ease in which her incisors split the peanut center. After twenty-nine egg-shaped M&M's, she places the folded bag into her backpack. She's still anxious about flying, but now there's her candy-caused achy stomach. To relax, she draws circles on her left forearm with her right index finger, can't stop from imagining a singed and trembling aircraft struck by lightning; a man with a snuck-on Luger shooting out every window in the cabin; the plane's fuselage split open by a mid-air iceberg. Her light touch stimulates bumps that rise up from her skin like a dainty mountain range—a crash landing will be impossible.

Myles's imagination works overtime to fill in the empty space in his brain where he wants her name to appear—Dolly? Ruth? Silisia? Chlöe? He looks over to see her in mid-incantation as she fingerprints her arm, talks to herself while sucking chewed M&M-remnants from between her teeth.

He thinks maybe they'll share a row, between them an empty seat of separation—let fate do the introductions—and they'll spend the cross-country flight moving beyond *What do you do?*'s, and *Traveling for why?*'s, and onto *Who could have predicted?*

On board the plane, the woman to Nicole's right has her hands clasped in prayer. She's asking Jesus to forgive her for how selfish she's being, taking this aircraft, instead of walking on bare feet across the country, as He walked barefoot for a very long time in Jerusalem, even though there was no concrete then, or cars, even, but still.

Nicole rolls her eyes, squeezes on headphones. She waits out the plane's delayed takeoff by studying the Safety on Board flight card, admiring the calm order of the cartoon passengers who plot a sure-fail escape with pleased half-smiles. Then she flips open SkyMall Magazine to a spread of pages that boast Gravity Defying Boots, the Portable Backyard Ice Rink, and Flybar™'s Elastomeric-Spring Pogo Stick.

Looking up, she sees a man shuffling to the toilet, scanning passengers. His unknotted shoelaces trailing like sine waves. Her eyes lock onto his for a brief moment before she looks down to see his hand squeezed around a bag of Skittles. She thinks: yum.

Over the loudspeaker: The pilot apologizes for getting a late start.

Sixteen minutes later, the plane lifts sharply. The cabin quickly cools, thin blankets are freed in plastic rips. A showing of linked seatbelts blare bright on the panel overhead with a *bing-bong*, while lavatory lights dim to dark. Outside of the curved windows, people turn to specks, cars appear Hot Wheels tiny.

After an hour there's a stomach-sinking jerk. The plane is yanked backwards by an invisible force.

Over the loudspeaker: The pilot apologizes for the turbulence.

Myles's next-seat-neighbor jerks awake, her body spasms as if suddenly electrocuted—a nightmare? Then she relaxes, stares straight ahead. Later, while wide awake, she yanks as an all-new electricity rides through her torso and arms.

For the next twenty minutes, Myles's anxiety skyrockets as he braces for her unpredictable shudders. To calm himself, he looks out of the window, soaks up the sky's relaxing ice blue, the cloud's calming grey white. Then the horrific happens: a phlegmy cough of black smoke erupts from the engine. Spills of inky smolder swim from beneath the plane's right wing.

The plane wobbles, drops, then steadies. The passengers moan in tandem, followed by a panic of screeches. Oxygen masks release, and dangle.

Over the loudspeaker: The pilot apologizes for the blown engine.

At varied volumes, the woman next to Nicole says, "gonna die. I'm gonna die. I'm gonna…"

Nicole pulls her cell phone from her jacket pocket, holds it out to the woman. "If you could maybe leave that as my outgoing message," Nicole says, "Since, you know, this is *only* happening to you."

The woman goes quiet—her eyes puzzle Nicole's reaction—then she raises her right hand and rakes at Nicole's eyes with her chewed finger nubs. Nicole slaps the attack off target, the woman buckles into sobs. "Fine," Nicole says. She puts her arm around the woman's shoulder and pulls her close.

A mechanical failure. Improper inspection. Maybe bad luck? When the left engine follows suit and mutates into a fireball, no one on board points a finger at why all of this is happening, or who's at fault.

The left wing flaps unnaturally until the engine breaks off and free-falls into the atmosphere. The wing starts to shred apart in a spike of wind-blown flame—half of it disappears in a snapshot, an eye blink. Crumbs of alloy sift behind in dusty metallic puffs.

Over the loudspeaker: The pilot apologizes for the disintegrated left wing.

The flight attendant labors to get the drink cart to the back of the plane. Then the plane hard-tilts, and the attendant is thrown across the laps of a married couple opposite Myles. Bottles of water go airborne, glance armrests, drunkenly promenade down the light-lined aisle. The married man and the married woman reach their arms around the attendant, hold her close. She returns the embrace. The unmanned drink cart staggers down the aisle, towards the front of the plane where it tips and stalls. A drawer opens: soft drinks spill out in a thudding aluminum clatter.

As the plane leaps down corrugated sheets of cirrus, the absurd force pins Myles to his seat-back. He fathoms discovering the name of the girl in 27C, filling in the blank during a brief conversation, an invite to dine. He fills his lungs with an oxygen mask blast, which makes him feel invincibly romantic. Loosing his seatbelt, he slips from his aisle seat. Thrust cinematically back, the aircraft's slant and earthward haste has him falling *up*. On his hurried streak to the plane's tail, he contorts in a frightening instant so his eyes—a cocktail of desire-fueled fear—lock onto hers. He abbreviates his flirtation to one word, a request, asking, *"DINNER!?"* as he flashes by.

Myles hits the rear of the plane with impossible force. His bones shatter like glass.

Nicole's fears are confirmed: the plane is a passenger missile.

A man somewhere on board starts vomiting. The cabin goes putrid with the nose-crinkling smell of reversed peristaltic waves.

She breathes weakly through her mouth, eyes closed, hands covering her ears. She is intent on timing the impact of the plane meeting ground by saying the word: Now.

"Now," she says. Waits. Tries to feel it. Tensing, she says, *"Now."*

"Now."

"Now."

Over the loudspeaker: The pilot apologizes for killing everyone.

Now.

Everything white, the newcomers glow with day-ready freshness. They walk aimlessly on a soft ground covered in clouds.

"Hello, I'm Myles," Myles says, approaching Nicole.

"I'm Nicole," Nicole says.

He nods, already knowing.

"I wanted those Skittles," she says. "They would have served as an effective gateway to my heart because of the gesture's romantic oddity."

"I was at fault for applying my own shyness and embarrassment onto others, as I did in your case," Myles tells her. "Though, in fairness, it often served to protect me from rejection."

"You have beautiful eyes," she says.

"I want to hold your hand," he says.

"This is going better than expected."
"This is unexpected."

A man—white mustache, combed back white hair—appears through a cloud. He introduces himself as Peter, then shouts to the sky, "Unplug the smoke machine! It's killing my throat." Then he laughs, because of course his throat isn't bothered, and of course there's no smoke machine, only clouds.

Peter welcomes everyone from American Airlines flight 201. He says, "When you're finished milling about"—pointing to a levitating, white doorway—"don't let the door hit you in the ass on your way in."

He shuffles off toward the cloud he came from.

"I want to understand," a woman says, the praying one from the plane.

Peter turns in her direction and says, "But you already do."

Myles and Nicole go through the door holding hands. Heaven opens up into a bustling piazza. The air like ozone—cool and crisp—they both feel wide-awake, their bodies refreshed and free of aches. Nicole leans in close, squeezes Myles's arm, says, "*Wow.*"

Their side-by-side homes are entangling as they arrive. Myles's home is strange-angled with odd-doorway'd rooms—the makings of his late-adolescent architecture fetish come to (after)life.

Nicole's home is enormous. It features impossibly sized, ceiling-free rooms that open to a cumulus rich sky. The pastel Nicole-in-Wonderland furniture is massive.

A few days pass when Myles says, "What's different is there are no advertisements."

Nicole says, "What's different is I don't need lotion for my hands."

"What's different is it's always room temperature."

"Unless you want it to not be room temperature."

"Totally."

"What's different is I'm no longer allergic to pineapple."

"What's different is my ambition is focused specifically on personal betterment."

"And no one ever acts like a butthole."

"What's different is I get to know everything if I want to know everything."

"What's different is I feel good all the time."

"What's different is I'm *happy.*"

Inseparable, it's weeks of woven limbs—Myles and Nicole buried under waves of goose down, their heads resting on the whopping fluffed pillows of Nicole's imagination.

"You're all I want in terms of another person. There's such a sense of completion," Myles says. "Plus you're completely bleeping hot."

A shocked pause.

"Holy bleep!" Myles says.

Nicole laughing, she says, "What the bleep? Hahah. You're bleeping kidding me! This is totally bleeped."

"Censorship!" Myles hollers, then, "I can't bleeping believe it!"

"This is bleepbucketry of the highest order!"

"What a crock of sheet."

"Fudge this noise!"

They nearly laugh themselves to death.

On their way to the market at twilight, Nicole spots the pilot surrounded by soul mates. He waves at them energetically, his joy absolute.

Without a loudspeaker: the pilot apologizes for not crashing a plane sooner.

That same temperatureless evening—the sky a bruise of still-blue black—Myles and Nicole snack on a flavor-packed Sunkist orange.

"I don't breathe anymore," Myles admits.

"Then how..." she starts, but instantly she understands, which spurs a sudden burst of other knowing. Nicole's mouth sinks into stressed frown. She stares down at the orange slices in her palm. The peel stripped away, she holds the three wedges out to Myles in a sort of pleading way.

It's an unspecified time without air, water, or food when Nicole shuffles in to see Myles on her enormous couch listening to *Calculus I in 20 Minutes* while he whittles a block of wood into a detailed Stockholm skyline.

He smiles at her and for a short while, she watches him work. Then she plucks a picnic basket from beneath the couch and eats: a pecan roll, eight pieces of salmon sashimi, a slice of German chocolate cake, a pork chop, a handful of risotto, six miniature tuna tacos, a filet mignon bacon burger, chicken Kiev, a pint of Tofutti coffee marshmallow swirl.

She's nine bites into an unsliced pepperoni pizza when Myles stops carving windows into a skyscraper and says, "Nicole?"

For three days, Myles finds the connected doors between their houses locked shut. He's stumped by his general feeling of glee in the face of Nicole's rejection. He exits the rhombus of his front door, knocks on the oversized of hers.

Nicole answers, pushes the golden mess of her hair away from her eyes. Myles's unsure "Hello?" is doused by her curtly asking, "*What?*"

"Here," he says, and presents her with a hand-carved wooden heart with a hole in the off-center. Inside the hole is a tiny wooden sculpture of Myles standing inside, pulling at the hole, trying to close it up.

"Do you?" she asks. "Because I don't. I don't *feel* anything."

She waits for his reaction. He's too stunned to offer one.

"Feeling all this *happy* is not feeling," she says. "There is nothing but pleasure. That's *not* a life!"

"It's a death," he says.

In a wide-open park, the spastic, jerking woman from the plane: sips water from her cupped hands; stacks a dozen wine glasses atop each other into a translucent tower; uses an X-ACTO knife to carve letters from a handwritten note; threads a needle on the first try.

The married couple from the plane and the flight attendant unlock their held hands to applaud vigorously.

After a curtsy, the unspastic, non-jerking woman lays on the ground until her smile turns into a soft frown of rest.

Next day, Myles goes to Nicole, who's so anxious she jumps when he eases his hands around her waist. "Just don't, okay?" she scolds, sheds his hands, turns. Her arms cross.

He waits for an explanation.

"Look, the plane hasn't crashed yet."

He sends her a puzzled look, but already her words are a virus spreading through his brain. She's told him, without speaking, that the plane's nose is a frozen instant from touch down, that Myles' life, his death, is on pause—he's now existing in his own, personal *Twilight Zone* episode and has imagined this Heaven in the millisecond before impact.

Nicole waits for her face to break open into a guilty, pained flood now that she's exposed a utopia-quaking loophole by digging her splinter of unhappiness under Myles' skin. It's just that before death Nicole had never been happy; then she came here and she was so impossibly happy. And now *this*. She digs her fingernails into her arm, for feeling, but there's no pain, there's nothing.

"I want to be the reason you allow yourself to be happy," Myles says. "But I don't want to share your doubt."

Myles thinks what he knows, bullies it into her thoughts: I was already a wet mess of misguided romantic splatter in the back of the plane when it crashed (or didn't yet).

Nicole's toes curl and uncurl in her shoes, her feet hurry into a Flintstones blur. She whirs past him, right out the door.

Nicole runs and runs but doesn't run out of breath. She finally collapses out of spite, her fists ball-peen against the soft ground. She thinks: *I've lost him.* Thinks, *What have I* done?

But, of course, she hasn't lost him—Myles is right behind her. His long strides mean he's upon her in seconds.

The religious woman from the plane strolls by in fishnets, a skimpy cocktail dress, six-inch heels. "Oh, you poor thing," she says, leaning down at the waist. She touches Nicole's cheek with a finger. "All this business of defining yourself by conflict is *over*."

Nicole turns away, again batters the ground with her fists, but nothing breaks.

"You could just go ahead and love him back," the woman says.

Nicole looks up at Myles, who's looking at her. He stands there wanting to matter, wanting to feel irreplaceable. Nicole looks at the woman who's teasing the tail of her white feather boa with red-painted fingertips.

"I thought death would give meaning to life," Nicole pleads.

"But life is that which gives meaning to life, sweetheart," the woman says.

"Then death gives meaning to nothing!"

The woman looks at Nicole, at Myles, at Nicole. "No, honey," the woman says, flicks the boa over her shoulder, "death gives *every*thing."

Adrian Todd Zuniga

Adrian Todd Zuniga is the host/creator of Literary Death Match (a literary event now featured in fifty-one cities worldwide), and the founding editor of *Opium Magazine*. His fiction has been featured in *Gopher Illustrated* and *Stymie*, and online at *Lost Magazine* and *McSweeney's*. He lives between Los Angeles and guest rooms all over Europe.

Readux

Readux Books: Series 2, № 8

ISBN: 978-3-944801-11-7

Cover illustration by Susann Stefanizen

Published by Readux Books
Sorauer Str. 16, 10997 Berlin, Germany

www.readux.net